The Marathon Race Mystery

BY ROBERT McNEAR

Illustrations by Jackie Rogers

Library of Congress Cataloging in Publication Data

McNear, Robert, (date)
The marathon race mystery.

(Solve-it-yourself)
Summary: The reader, a school reporter and amateur detective, overhears a suspicious conversation in a sporting goods store that may affect an upcoming marathon. A course of action must be decided on right away.
1. Plot-your-own stories. 2. Children's stories, American. [1. Mystery and detective stories. 2. Plot-your-own stories] I. Rogers, Jackie, ill. II. Title. III. Series.
PZ7.M478794Mar 1985 [Fic] 84-16395
ISBN 0-8167-0444-9 (lib. bdg.)
ISBN 0-8167-0445-7 (pbk.)

Printed in the United States of America.

10 9 8 7 6 5 4 3 2 1

The Marathon Race Mystery

Warning!

In this story, *you* are the detective! *You* must find the clues, follow the leads, and try to solve the mystery.

But do not read this book from beginning to end. Start on page 1, and keep reading till you come to a choice. After that, the story is up to you. Your decisions will take you from page to page.

Think carefully before you decide. Some choices will lead you to further clues. But other choices may bring about a quick end to your investigation—and to you!

Whatever happens, you can always go back to the beginning and start again. Best of luck in your investigation.

1

In 490 B.C., the ancient Greeks won a fierce battle over the Persians at a place called Marathon. The Greek forces sent a runner back from the battlefield to announce the victory—a messenger named Pheidippides, who raced about twenty-five miles without stopping and voiced the news with his last breath.

In 1896, to honor this great feat, the Olympic long-distance run was called a "marathon." Twenty-five runners ran the first race.

Marathon can still be found on the map, but to most of us the word marathon means a footrace of 26 miles 385 yards—one of the highlights of the modern Olympic Games.

Today, many cities and towns host marathon races. Those races are usually the athletic highlight of the year, long remembered after the last footsore runner has finished.

Tony's

You are known to your friends and classmates as a successful amateur detective, for you have solved—or helped to solve—many mysteries around your school and in your neighborhood. You are also one of your school newspaper's top reporters, and your editor has chosen you to cover your town's upcoming marathon.

Because the race will be run tomorrow morning, Sunday, you decide to go down to Tiny's Sporting Goods Store. It may be the perfect place to get background information on some of the local runners.

The owner of the store may be called "Tiny," but that's like calling Lake Superior a puddle. The man is 6 feet 6 inches tall and weighs more than 260 pounds. When he stepped onto the football field as a college player, members of the other team wished they could be playing gin rummy. Tiny has become a pretty good friend of yours over the past year.

Tiny sees you as you enter the crowded store. "Hi. Covering the race for the paper?"

"Yes, I am. How many are running this year?" you ask.

"About five thousand, I think. And right now it looks like they're all shopping here for gear. Excuse me for a minute."

Tiny moves off to wait on customers, and you wander through the store and head toward the running-gear department. The department is crowded with customers—marathon runners of all ages, sizes, and shapes.

At a rack of camping gear, you pause for a moment. You can hear two men talking on the other side of the rack, but you can't see them. What you can see is the hand of one of the men as he reaches for a backpack. He is wearing an enormous ring, with a distinctive design.

"We're all registered for the race," says the man to his companion. "And this backpack"—he lowers his voice, but you edge closer—"should be big enough to hide the head."

"The head," the other man says under his breath. "I've waited years for this."

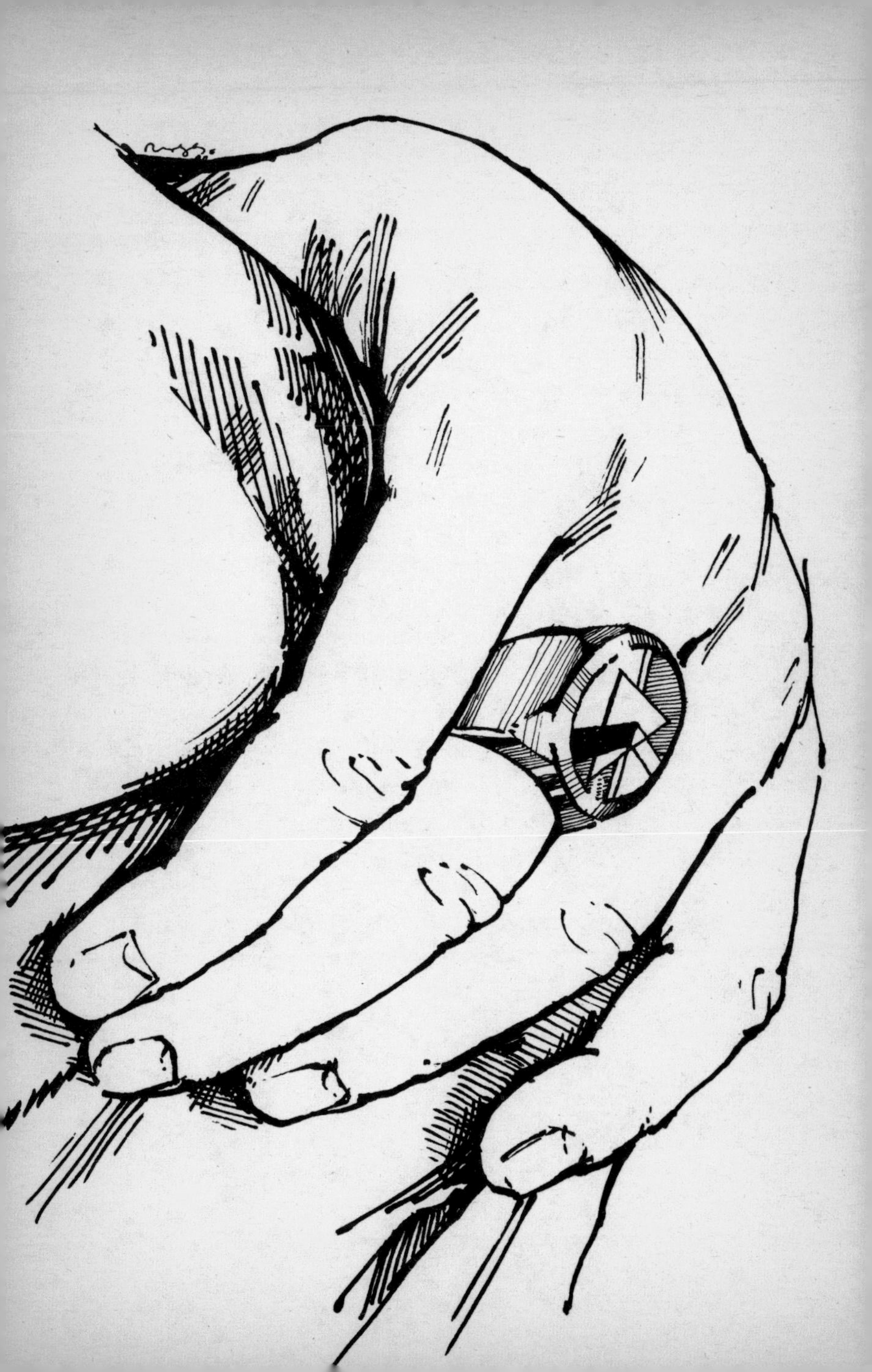

6

Suddenly a friend spots you and comes over to tell you about the new computer at school. You don't want to be impolite, but after a few minutes you excuse yourself. You step out quickly from behind the clothes rack to get a look at the two men, but they are gone.

Your first thought is to go to the police, but what would you tell them? Something about a backpack big enough to hide a head? Whose head? And who were those two men? There may be a time to go to the police, you think, but not right away. You need to know more. You seem to have three possible courses of action.

One: The men have already bought the backpack and left the store. Maybe the cashier at the register would remember the man if you described his ring. Or maybe the man is a regular customer and Tiny knows him. Perhaps one of the men paid for the backpack with a credit card, or produced some kind of identification so he could pay by check. If so, you'd have some information to use to begin to track them down.

Two: Since you know the men have already registered for the race, perhaps you should go to the marathon registration office and try to track them that way. You could describe the ring and hope that someone noticed it. It certainly caught your eye. Someone in the office might remember the ring *and* the man who wore it.

Three: You could go to the public library. The design of the ring looked Arabic or Middle Eastern to you. Maybe some research would give you a solid lead.

Since overhearing that strange conversation, you realize that your sports assignment could turn out to be an entirely different kind of story.

If you think you should go over and talk to Tiny and the cashier, turn to page 10.

If you think you should go to the marathon registration office, turn to page 11.

If you think you should go to the public library, turn to page 18.

8

from page 73

You know that the only sensible thing to do is to continue with your investigation. The criminals know you are onto their plan. They are also too smart to give up that easily. They will most likely try some other way to pull off the Ha-tep job. But how?

Tiny thinks that there is only one other possibility. The only underground entrance to the museum, other than the electrical tunnels, would be the water tunnels. Back to the Department of Public Works you go.

When you review the plumbing- and water-service plans for the museum, you can see quite clearly that there are two big water tunnels that go from the river to the museum. You ask a DPW technician to explain the tunnels on the map for you.

"There are two tunnels going to that spot, for one simple reason," the man explains. "One tunnel carries all of the museum's water from the river to the building. The other one is left empty so technicians can walk through to check water levels and to make sure everything is in good working order."

"You mean people can actually walk through this tunnel here on the right? Just walk from the river to the museum underground?" you ask.

"That's exactly right," says the technician.

That's all you need to know. You have no time to lose.

You ask the technician where the closest available phone is. He points you down the hall to the first door on your right. When you get to the phone, you dial Lieutenant Duffy's office and explain to him how to catch the thieves.

On marathon Sunday, you stand by the finish line with pad, pencil, and radio in hand. At the finish of the race, you hear on the radio that three men have been arrested for the attempted robbery of the famous Egyptian artifact. You've done it. You have saved the head of Ha-tep and got the best marathon story ever.

THE END

from page 7/from page 57

At the cash register, Tiny is wrapping up a pair of running shoes. After motioning to him to come over and talk with you, you ask him why two men who were going to run in the marathon would buy a backpack. He explains that many people who run in the race like to show off by running in special outfits, one of which is a set of combat fatigues with a backpack.

You quickly tell him what you overheard. Then you sketch the design of the ring on the back of a blank sales slip. Tiny and the cashier both look at the sketch, then shake their heads.

"Sorry," says Tiny. "All I can think of is that the ring looks Egyptian. If not that, it's certainly from somewhere in the Middle East. I have a friend named Hazan who might be able to help you track it down. Here's how you can find him."

As Tiny writes down the address for you, you decide to get in touch with Mr. Hazan.

Turn to page 15.

from page 7

Remembering what the strange ring looked like, you visit the marathon office and observe their registration procedure.

The race officials review applications on the spot, then either accept or reject each applicant. If the runner is accepted, he or she is issued a number. Runners must display their numbers on both the front and back of their shirts.

The office is crowded the day before the race. You wait patiently until you can talk to the officials at the registration desks, some of whom you know from your coverage of past races. When it's finally your turn to talk to an official, you come right to the point.

"Have you registered a runner wearing a ring like this?" you ask, showing each of them a drawing you have made.

You show this drawing to four different officials. The first three shake their heads, but the fourth official looks long and hard. He thinks for a moment.

"Yes," he says, "I registered him this morning. At first I didn't recognize the design from your drawing. I can't connect the ring with a name, but I can tell you this much—I saw him leave in a van with another man. A strange-looking van."

"What was strange about the van?" you ask.

"Pyramids," he says. "Pyramids painted on the sides of the van."

You thank the official, then think about your next step. To ride your bike around town looking for this strange van could take days. You might never find it. Suddenly you get a better idea.

One by one, you call your fellow reporters on the newspaper and ask them to keep their eyes open. You ask them to call you if they see such a van. Sure enough, later that afternoon, you get a call.

The reporter saw the van pulled over by a police officer, near the museum. You ask the reporter if she remembers the license plate or model of the van.

"As a matter of fact, since it looked like the van you were talking about, I wrote down the license-plate number," she says. "It was one of those personalized plates you can get if you pay extra money. It had only numbers, no letters, and the numbers looked like a phone number."

"What were they?" you ask.

"421-8371."

You thank your observant friend and hang up the phone. The obvious thing to do would be to call the number. But there is something strange about this.

Why would a van have a phone number on its license plate? You study the numbers carefully. Then your detective's instincts go to work for you. On the dial of the phone, the letters that correspond to the numbers on the license plate could spell something interesting. The groups of letters for 421-8371 are: GHI, ABC, TUV, DEF, and PRS. (The number 1 has no letters on the phone dial.) But what could such a code be?

After staring at the many possible combinations of letters, you realize that by taking one letter from each group, you can spell several different words. But one word that spells an ancient name intrigues you the most: HA-TEP.

You don't even have to dial the number. You know that there is an exhibit at your town's museum on the art of ancient Egypt. You have read in the newspaper that the highlight of the display is the world-famous bust of Ha-tep, a queen of ancient Egypt. You could go to the museum to see if this mystery van shows up. Or you could go to your town's local office of the Department of Motor Vehicles to try to find out who has registered the van.

If you think you should check out the museum, turn to page 42.

If you think you should go to the Department of Motor Vehicles to find out who registered the van, turn to page 83.

from page 10

Tiny's friend, Mr. Hazan, lives in the penthouse of an old apartment building. The elevator reminds you of a parrot's cage, with wires running all around you. After a few squeals and a few lurches, the elevator lets you off at the top floor. No one answers your knock on Hazan's door. But the door is open a crack, and you walk in quietly.

Your first thought is that Hazan's mother would be furious if she saw this apartment. Things are sticking out of all the drawers, and stuff is lying on the floor. The room is an absolute mess. Then you realize that someone has searched this room.

Before you can examine the room yourself, you hear footsteps behind you. You turn and see a man wearing a business suit.

"I'm with the police," the man says, showing his badge. "Lieutenant Duffy. Who are you?"

You tell the lieutenant who you are, then tell him all about the entire conversation you overheard in Tiny's store. Lieutenant Duffy's eyes narrow; then he smiles. "Sounds like a joke to me. People don't run around with heads in backpacks."

"Lieutenant, may I ask what brought you here?"

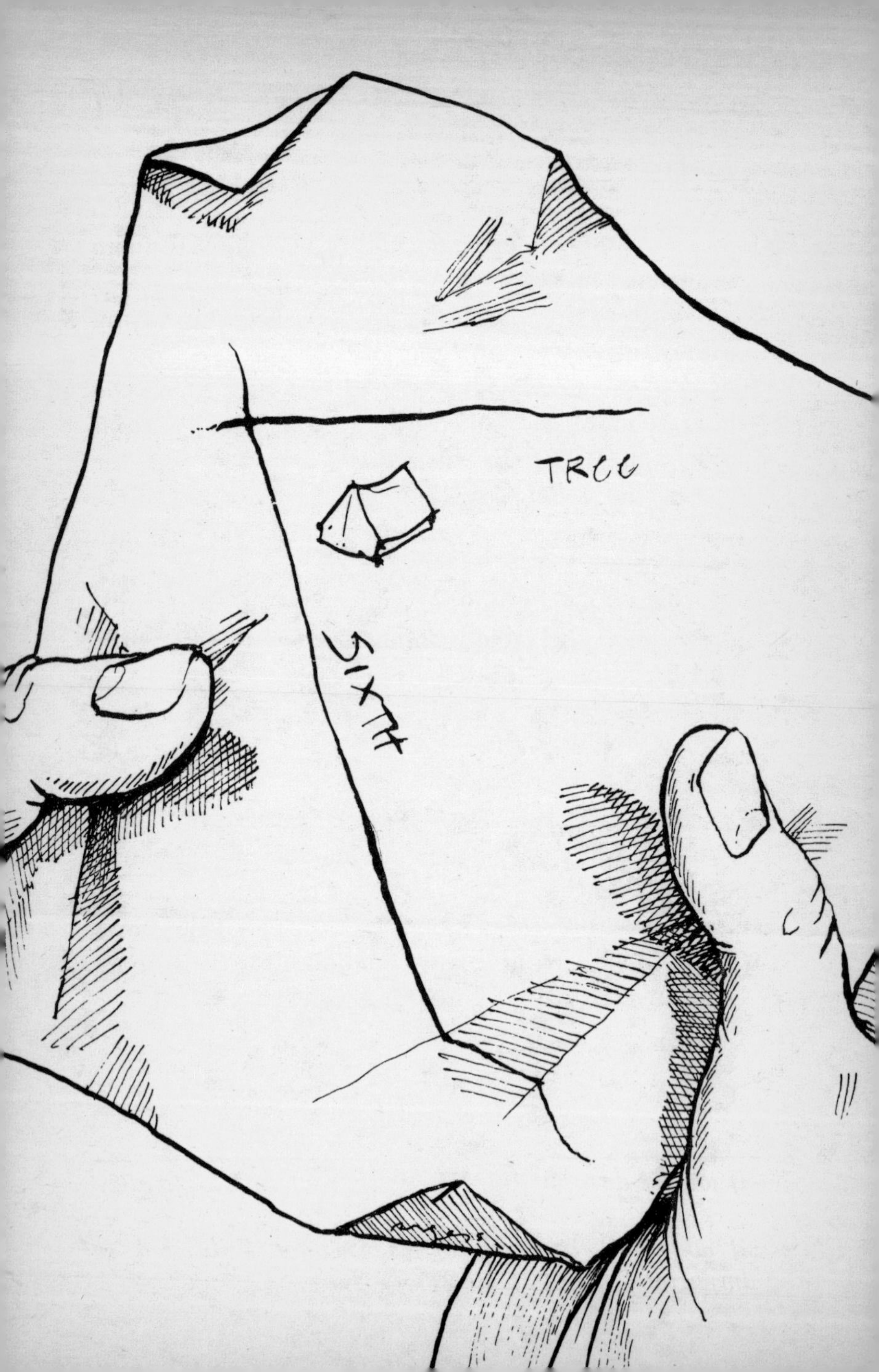
TREE
SIXTH

"An anonymous phone call. The caller said there was trouble here."

With that, the police officer begins walking around the apartment. From time to time he writes in his notebook. Suddenly you notice something on the living-room table—a piece of paper sticking out from under a book. Perhaps this was overlooked by whoever searched the room. You pick it up and take a quick look at it. The words SIXTH, TREE, and some kind of tent are drawn on the paper. You pass it to the lieutenant.

"Doesn't make any sense to me," says Duffy.

Also on the table is a matchbox with the words NILE RESTAURANT printed on the cover.

"What do you suppose happened here?" you ask.

"Maybe a burglary," says Duffy. "First thing to do is find the fellow who lives here."

"I think I'll be running along," you say. Lieutenant Duffy puts the drawing and the matchbox cover into his pocket.

"Okay. But, listen," he says. "You're a little young to be sticking your nose into anything dangerous. Here's my card. If you need me, call."

If you decide to go to the Nile Restaurant, turn to page 32.

If you think the drawing Lieutenant Duffy took is important, turn to page 21.

from page 7

If you can find out more about the Middle East, you might find a clue about the strange ring. You go to your town's library and start reading. The information on the religions of ancient Egypt interests you the most.

At various times, the Egyptians worshiped many different gods and goddesses, and each god had a group of followers who believed in that particular god above all others. There was the cult of Osiris, king and judge of the dead; Ra, the sun god; Amon, a great god of one of the Egyptian dynasties; and Ha-tep, an important queen of Egypt later made a goddess. You learn that each of these cults had a symbol, which appeared on all the writings about them. These pictures give you your first solid clue.

For the rest of the afternoon, you read all you can on the history of ancient Egypt. All you find is one more possible clue. At the end of an article on the religions of ancient Egypt is a list of books on the subject, including *Worship in Old Egypt*, by Peter Andrews. The author's name sounds familiar. Where have you heard it?

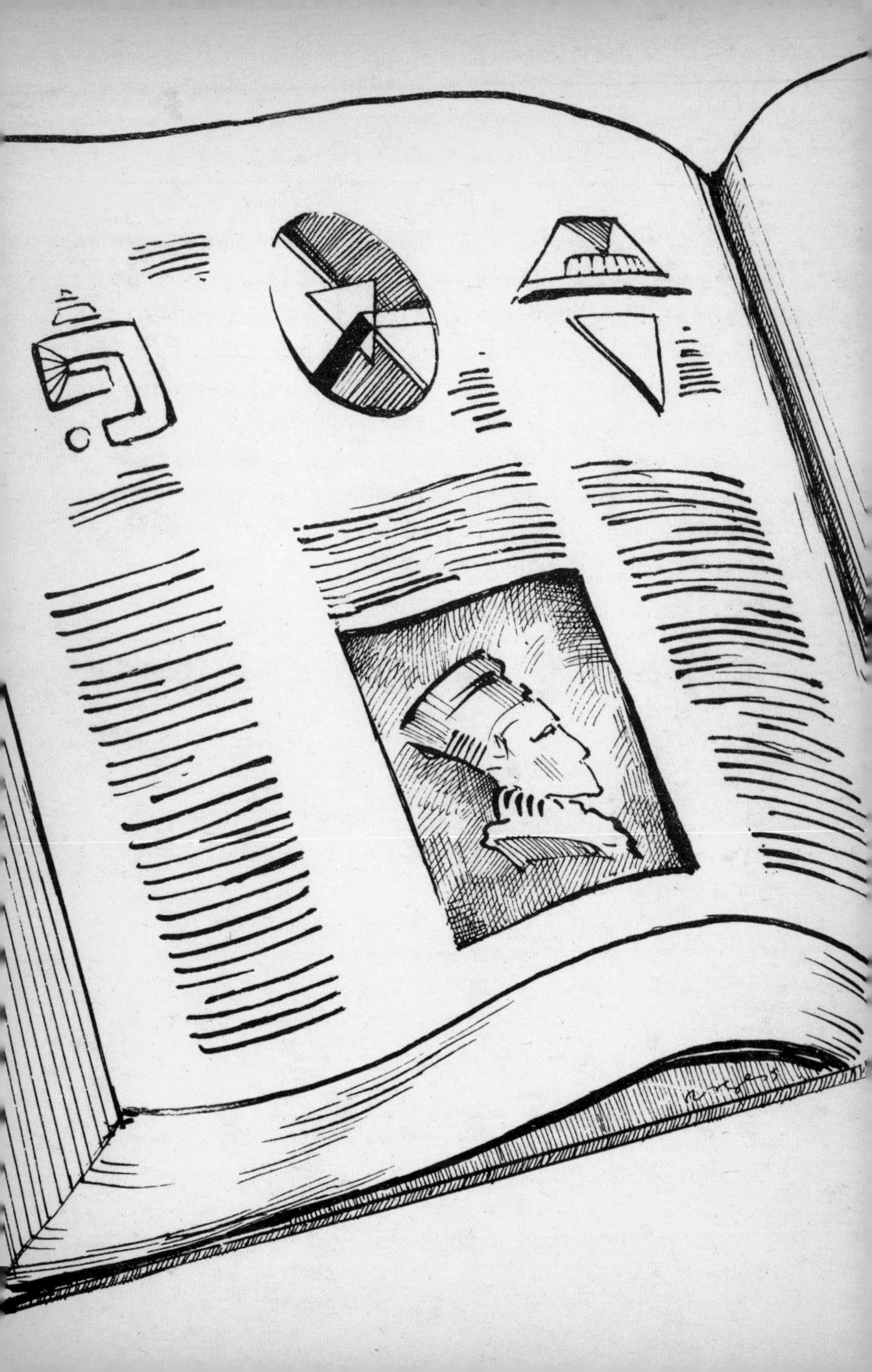

Of course! Peter Andrews is running in the marathon right here in your town, and you remember something about him from covering the race last year. Peter Andrews, a local runner, nearly won last year's race. And you remember hearing that besides being a great runner, Andrews is also an expert on ancient Egypt and a part-time curator at your town's museum.

You could try to contact Peter Andrews. Or you could visit the museum, another good source of information on ancient Egypt.

If you think you should contact Peter Andrews, turn to page 27.

If you think you should visit the museum, turn to page 42.

from page 17

You were right to consider the slip of paper more carefully. After thinking for most of the day, your mystery-solving abilities finally pay off. You realize that the drawing must refer to the corner of 6th Street and Pine Street (the only street in your town that crosses 6th and is named after a tree). You decide to check out that corner first thing tomorrow morning, the day of the marathon race.

Sunday morning, when you get to the corner of 6th and Pine, it all makes sense. On that corner is your town's biggest and best jewelry store. Bars over the windows and thick steel doors protect a fortune in jewels inside.

Just as you saw in the drawing, a small tent stands in the intersection, the kind used by city workers to cover an open hole in the street. You assume that the hole leads to a tunnel. While the marathon race is on, and while everyone's attention is diverted, thieves will probably try to rob your town's best jewelry store—from below.

The lieutenant has warned you about danger, but you know you can depend on Tiny for help if you ever need it. There is a pay phone on the corner, and you phone them both. Neither is in, so you leave word for each of them. You give them the street address and ask them to meet you there. Hanging up the phone, you wonder what your next move should be. You're alone, and the possibilities for danger are everywhere. You must be cautious. You go over to the hole in the street and try to see inside. No harm in going down in the hole and looking around a *little*, you think.

You go down in the hole and peer carefully down a tunnel in the direction of the jewelry store. Without a flashlight, it's difficult to see in the darkness. The only sources of light are the dim electric light bulbs placed every twenty feet or so. The cold underground air sends a chill through your body.

All the electrical wiring you see suggests that the tunnel is used by the utility company. Before you know it, you arrive at what must be an underground door to the jewelry store. The name of the store and some numbers—maybe utility-company codes—are painted on the door. Nothing seems tampered with. Gathering your courage, you investigate other connecting tunnels around the store. Everything is in order. Were you mistaken about a break-in?

Suddenly you come upon an iron door covered with signs like KEEP OUT, DO NOT ENTER, and DANGER. You have to follow all possible leads, so you carefully open the door and peak inside. The room seems to be just a storage room. It is filled with pipes and wires. You step into the room.

With a thunderous crash, the door swings shut behind you. You are trapped.

Time passes. You try yelling, and pounding on the door. A small light bulb hangs from the ceiling, and in the dim light you watch the hands on your wrist watch. Then you hear something.

At first you think it's your imagination. Has the door moved an inch? Is someone trying to open it from the other side?

You want to shout. The fingers of two hands appear, opening the door wider and wider. The fingers are huge, larger than any you have ever seen. Then you see the giant hands. Your knees feel weak. Summoning every ounce of courage, you prepare to meet this threat.

"Hey," says Tiny, opening the door wide. "You're going to miss the marathon race."

For a moment Tiny becomes the world's largest pillow as you throw your arms around him. A moment later, Lieutenant Duffy appears with some of his officers. The police officers fan out, covering the underground route around the store. Soon they return, shaking their heads.

"Not a thing, Lieutenant," one officer says. "Clean as a whistle."

"So much for that," says Lieutenant Duffy.

"I thought I was onto something," you say. "Sorry I wasted your time."

"You weren't the only one who called," the lieutenant says. "Someone else called about the same time."

"Really?" you ask. "That makes all the difference in the world."

"Sure does," Tiny says. "Don't you see what that means?"

"It means that someone else also wanted the police here, probably so the police wouldn't get in the way of the real crime. They'd be down here crawling through empty tunnels."

"What real crime? Do you mean that stuff about the head?" Lieutenant Duffy asks.

"I do," you say.

Lieutenant Duffy then gets a message on his walkie-talkie. A guard at the museum is missing, the guard from the gallery containing the head of Ha-tep.

"There's our answer," you say. "The race course runs right by the museum."

"Let's get to the museum," the Lieutenant says. "Pronto."

"Wait a minute," you say, looking at your watch. "Most of the race has already passed the museum. Ten to one the head is no longer there."

"Maybe we can pick up the trail from the museum," says Lieutenant Duffy.

"Or," you say, "we can go to the finish line of the marathon, and let the head come to us."

If you decide to get to the museum as quickly as you can, turn to page 48.

If you think you'll have a better chance at the finish line, turn to page 38.

from page 20

Peter Andrews is listed in the phone book, and you dial the number.

"Hello?"

You introduce yourself and ask with whom you're speaking.

"I am Peter's uncle," the voice answers.

When you ask if you can speak with Peter, the uncle says that his nephew is not home. He is out practicing for the marathon. He should be running in the park now, the man tells you.

"Do you know what he was wearing when he left?" you ask.

"Yes, he was wearing a blue warmup suit with two yellow stripes down the side," his uncle says.

You leave for the park, watching for a young man wearing a blue warmup suit. Workers have already painted a blue stripe down the middle of the road that runs through the park. Potholes have been filled in. At certain places bleachers have been erected, so that without blocking the race course thousands of spectators may watch the runners pass by.

Seeing lots of runners doing warmup exercises, you begin to feel the excitement of this great event. But you don't see Peter Andrews. Later in the afternoon, as you slowly make your way home, you decide to stop in at the runner's house. On your way, you notice a taxi pull up to a street corner nearby.

Suddenly, a young man is pushed out the rear door of the taxi and falls to the ground. As the taxi roars away, the man slowly gets up. His warmup suit is unbuttoned, and his eyes are filled with fear. As you help him to his feet, you realize that he is Peter Andrews.

As you lead him over to a nearby bench, you introduce yourself. He says he remembers you from your coverage of last year's race. But now he has a strange story to tell you.

A half hour ago, he says, he was loosening up for the marathon when a taxi pulled up alongside him. A man with a gun gestured to Peter to get into the cab. There was no way to refuse. For a while the taxi drove around the city. Peter was told to face out the window as they drove. The man with the gun told Peter, "Don't run in the marathon race. If you do, your life will be in danger." Then the man ordered the driver to slow down, and he pushed Peter out the door.

As you sit on the bench, you glance across the street. You notice a man on the opposite sidewalk, leaning against an iron fence and pretending to read a book. He has a scruffy mustache and the beginnings of a beard.

30

"Peter," you say, "you almost came in first last year out of all the thousands of runners, right?"

"Yes," he says. "I came in third. And this year I think I can win."

He seems determined to race, in spite of the threat.

You say, "I remember Karl Sanders came in first. Who came in second?"

"George Fennimore."

"So if you don't race this year, Sanders and Fennimore might feel a little more comfortable about their chances."

"Oh, no," says Peter. "They couldn't have anything to do with this."

"Don't be too sure," you tell Peter. Then you show him your drawing of the symbol of the cult of Ha-tep. "Does this mean anything to you?"

Peter begins to fidget nervously. "Where did you get that?" he asks.

"It's the symbol for the cult of Ha-tep," you tell him.

"You have . . . Don't . . . I mean . . . " Peter stammers, getting to his feet. "I have to go now."

"What's the matter, Peter?" you ask. "Is it something about this drawing?"

"I have to go. Really. Thanks for your help."

"Do me a favor, Peter. And do yourself a favor. Tell the police about what happened—about the cab, I mean. Do it now. I'll help in any way I can, but you must tell the police."

"Okay. Good-bye," Peter says, shaking your hand. In a moment he is off, jogging down the street.

What's going on here? The drawing clearly unnerved Peter, as much as the cab ride and the threat. Does the ring have anything to do with the marathon race? Is Sanders involved? Is Fennimore?

Again you notice the man who had been watching you and Peter. With Peter gone, the man is now walking away in the opposite direction. What should you do?

If you think you should investigate Sanders and Fennimore, turn to page 56.

If you think you should follow the unknown man, turn to page 40.

from page 17

The Nile Restaurant is down by the river, in a part of town you don't know very well. When you get there, you find that the Nile looks more like a fancy diner than a restaurant. Yet it is dark inside, and strange flute music is playing from somewhere in the back. You walk over to the counter and sit down.

Are you wasting your time here? Lieutenant Duffy thought the entire conversation you overheard was a joke. You order a soda and look around the room. Most of the customers speak a strange language and seem to be from the Middle East. Suddenly a man sits down on the stool next to you and orders shish kebab. Soon his food arrives, and he begins to eat heartily. When you notice a ring on his left hand, however, your heart almost skips a beat.

"I'm afraid you spilled your soda," the man says politely, reaching for his napkin. You help clean up the spill on the counter.

"Sorry," you say.

The ring—the same ring you saw back at Tiny's! Is this the same man? You take a deep breath and try to calm down.

Another man makes his way toward the counter. He is wearing a business suit and a fez—a traditional hat of the eastern Mediterranean. The man with the fez whispers into the ear of the man sitting next to you, but you can still make out what he says.

"The Dixie Warehouse. Eight o'clock tonight."

Then the man with the fez quietly leaves the restaurant.

Now you have a real lead. But should you go to the Dixie Warehouse right away? Or should you go to the county clerk's office to try and find out who owns the warehouse?

If you think you should go to the Dixie Warehouse, turn to page 35.

If you think you should go to the county clerk's office, turn to page 54.

from page 34/from page 79

You go directly to the Dixie Warehouse and try to get inside. But all the doors are locked. As you wander quietly around outside, you notice an eerie light glowing from a third-story window. Spotting an old wooden ladder lying on top of a pile of sand, you pick up the ladder and try to lean it against the building. The ladder is a bit too heavy for you, however, and it falls against the wall.

Did anyone inside hear the noise? Should you run? After a few minutes of silence, you decide that either no one heard the noise, or there is no one inside. You adjust the ladder and climb up to the glowing third-story window. What you see inside is almost too much to believe.

More than thirty men are gathered in a circle in the middle of the wide warehouse floor. In the middle of the circle is a platform covered with a golden cloth. As you peer from the darkness outside, the men bow and chant, their eyes fixed on the empty space in the middle of the platform. They chant something that sounds like "hottup" or "haatay," as if speaking to the empty platform. "Ha-tep"—that's what it is, the name of the ancient Egyptian queen; a sculpture of her head is on display at the town's museum.

Away from the circle stands a big man with a long scar on his cheek. He seems to be the leader.

They are worshiping something that belongs on the platform, but what?

The head! It must be the head you heard about in the store. The mysterious head is supposed to be on the platform. The head that will somehow end up in a backpack during tomorrow's marathon race is destined for the center of the platform, to be worshiped by this circle of followers.

Who are these people? You might be able to find out by going to the county clerk's office to look up the name of the owner of the warehouse. Or you could go to the real-estate office where a friend of yours works, to see if anyone is trying to buy or sell the building.

If you think you should go to the county clerk's office, turn to page 54.

If you think you should go to the real-estate office, turn to page 85.

from page 26

When you arrive at the finish line, a large crowd has already gathered to wait for the runners to complete the race. You make your way to the front of the crowd for a better view.

In the distance, the lead runners soon appear. Around you are Tiny, Lieutenant Duffy, and his officers. The runners come nearer. A band begins to play. Television cameras are poised to record the great moment. People in the crowd lean forward, ready to urge on their favorites.

"The head will come to us," you say to Tiny. "All we have to do is be patient. From what I overheard in your store, we *know* they will try to make their escape with the head in a backpack. If they tried to rob the museum and escape on any old city street, they would attract a lot of attention, running where there is no race. But moving with the other runners, some of whom are wearing eye-catching costumes, they would look quite ordinary, except for one small detail."

"What's that?" the lieutenant asks. "Do you mean the strange ring?"

"No," you say. "The strange ring would be too difficult to spot. But a bulge in a backpack wouldn't be so hard to see. Let's keep our eyes open."

A few minutes after the lead runners cross the finish line, you see what you're looking for.

"Unless that runner is the Hunchback of Notre Dame, I think you might want to have a few words with him and his friend as soon as they cross the finish line," you tell the lieutenant. "Then I'd better write up my story. I may have missed most of the race, but catching the robbers of a priceless object is a good story, too, and I want to get it to my editor on time."

You have solved the marathon-race mystery.

THE END

from page 31

The man who had been watching you and Peter walks north along the street bordering the park. You follow him, staying close enough to keep him in sight but far enough away not to be obvious. Four blocks later the man enters Cityview Apartments, one of the fancy buildings overlooking the park. You quicken your pace.

You enter the lobby just as the man gets into an elevator. Above the elevator door is an indicator showing the floor the elevator is passing. The indicator climbs to the top floor (the sixteenth) and then stops. There is a building directory on one side of the lobby, and a quick look shows two occupants on the sixteenth floor: an L. Jasper in 16A and a W. Rush in 16B.

You notice that the man at the desk is watching you. Throwing him a smile, you walk back outside and look up. Then you look over to the park. From the sixteenth floor, you realize, your man has a great view of your town—a great view of tomorrow's marathon race.

You cross the street and wait on the sidewalk. After half an hour the mystery man comes out and walks two blocks south to a pay phone. This time he wears a different jacket, hat, and pants. He must have changed his clothes upstairs, but the mustache and the stubble on his face make his identity all too obvious. He closes the glass door behind him, and you can see him taking a piece of paper out of his pocket.

Then he places a call and talks for a while. He leaves the phone booth and heads back to the apartment house.

You are still on the other side of the street. After he passes you, you make for the phone booth. On the floor of the booth you notice a crumpled piece of paper. You smooth it out and read the phone number: 555-2198.

In the last hour or so you have learned two things about this man: His name is probably either L. Jasper or W. Rush, and for one reason or another, he doesn't like to use his own telephone.

You wonder if Peter has contacted the police. Perhaps you should phone him and find out. Or should you follow the lead of this new phone number—a phone call the man didn't want to make from his own apartment?

If you think you should follow the phone-number lead, turn to page 49.

If you think you should contact Peter, turn to page 45.

from page 14/from page 20/from page 83

The museum in your town stands in the park. In the front of the museum is a parking lot. An artificial lake borders the building to the north, trees and lawn stretch to the south, and along the back is a paved road winding through the park. As you park your bike in front of the museum, you realize that tomorrow the road in the back will be filled with marathon runners on their way to the finish line.

Like many art museums, the one in your town houses a permanent collection and, from time to time, special exhibits on loan from other collections or museums. Today, a banner flies in front of the museum announcing its latest special exhibit: ART FROM ANCIENT EGYPT.

Entering the museum, you ignore the permanent collection and go directly to the new Egyptian exhibit. You are nearly alone as you walk through the galleries. At the end of the main hall is a solitary display. Lights from the ceiling shine on a glass case. Not far from the case stands a guard.

As you move closer, your heart beats faster. Inside the case is a golden bust of a woman. On the glass, a card reads HA-TEP, QUEEN OF EGYPT, 1372–1350 B.C. ON LOAN FROM THE BERLIN MUSEUM.

For a moment you can recall the man's voice back at Tiny's store.

"The head. I've waited years for this."

Did he mean Ha-tep's head? You regard the stone bust in the case.

What should you do? Go to the police and tell them of your suspicion that Ha-tep's head will be stolen during the marathon race? Or see a friend of yours, Arthur Manning, a television newsman? Manning has been helpful to you and your school's paper in the past. If you explain the situation to him, he might get a camera crew to cover the museum during the race. That way you could get any possible trespassers on videotape.

If you think you should see the police, turn to page 74.

If you think you should see Arthur Manning, the TV newsman, turn to page 76.

from page 41

Once again you call Peter's house. You know that Peter lives with his uncle, who is an important businessman in town. His uncle answers the phone.

"Peter is not home," the uncle tells you. "He . . . uh . . . he had some business at his office."

On a Saturday? What business would he have on the Saturday before the big race? And why did the uncle say Peter was out running last time? The uncle has changed his story.

You find this news alarming and you go over to the uncle's apartment, hoping to get a straight answer face to face. The uncle is having coffee in the kitchen. He appears ill at ease.

"Peter phoned and said he is staying with friends," the uncle explains. You notice that his eyes do not meet yours.

"Did Peter tell you about the threat?" you ask the uncle. "About not running in the marathon?"

The uncle does not answer you. Instead he says, "I'm sorry, but I have a business date I must keep. I'll tell Peter you are looking for him."

You know there is something wrong, but there is not much more you can do. You say good-bye and leave.

But you can do one thing. You cross the street and wait for the uncle to leave for his "appointment." In a few minutes, Peter's uncle appears with a suitcase, and you follow him to a bank. He enters, and you follow.

Waiting by a counter, you notice the uncle talking to a banker. Peter's uncle and the banker go into a closed office. When the uncle reappears, still carrying the suitcase, he walks directly to the front door. The suitcase looks heavier than it did before.

Has Peter been kidnapped? If he has been, why was he released earlier? Has his uncle just withdrawn money for ransom? If so, he has probably been told not to report the kidnapping or Peter will be harmed, or killed. He may also have been told to get money, probably in small bills, and to wait for a phone call telling him where to deliver it.

The uncle returns to his apartment, leaving you to think about this serious situation.

You are tempted to call the police. The uncle would probably deny there has been a kidnapping. And it is really *his* decision whether or not to call the police. After all, it is Peter, his nephew, whose life is at stake.

Should you confront the uncle and tell him what you know? At least the uncle might possess some clue, for he certainly must have talked to the kidnappers.

Or should you check out the man—whatever his name might be—on the sixteenth floor of the building overlooking the park? Somehow he is involved, and he might lead you to Peter.

If you think you should confront the uncle, turn to page 118.

If you think you should check out the man on the sixteenth floor, turn to page 52.

from page 26

Lieutenant Duffy escorts you and Tiny out to his patrol car and tells the officer in the driver's seat to hightail it to the museum.

You arrive at the museum in time to see a few exhausted runners passing by on their way to the finish line, only a few miles away.

"At least there are still some runners this far back," you say to the lieutenant. "That may be a good sign."

Tiny, the lieutenant, and you run to the entrance of the museum and make your way to the Egyptian exhibit.

There, standing bare, is the pedestal that once held the famous bust of Ha-tep. The head is gone!

"They must be well up near the finish line by now," Tiny says.

"If not well on their way out of town," you add.

"I'll have to alert the authorities in the surrounding towns," says the lieutenant. "Looks like the crooks have fooled everyone, including us."

THE END

from page 41

The easiest way to run down a phone number is... to phone the number. The man you were following called that number, not from a private phone but from a pay phone. Suspicious, indeed!

You drop a coin into the slot and dial the number.

"Gilroy Taxi Service," comes the voice over the phone.

You replace the receiver and reach for the phone book hanging in the booth. The Gilroy Taxi Service is located on Second Avenue, which is not far from where you are.

You remember that Peter had been taken for a ride in a taxi, at which time a man had threatened him, telling him not to run in the marathon race. It could have been a Gilroy taxi. Later that afternoon, you ride your bike out to the taxi service.

Watching from across the street, you get an idea. You leave your bike across the street from the taxi service and walk down Second Avenue. You plan to hail the first Gilroy Taxi that comes along and ask to be taken downtown. That way you can engage the driver in conversation.

Before long a Gilroy cab comes along, and you flag it down. You hop into the back seat and tell the driver, "Downtown, please."

2.25

"I noticed you back there," the driver says, "watching our taxi office."

"Watching your taxi office?" you say, trying to sound casual. "I was waiting for a friend."

"Your friend must work for the taxi company," says the driver in an unpleasant tone.

"I was waiting for a friend," you repeat. "Hey, this isn't the way to downtown."

"Never said it was," the driver replies.

You notice a stoplight ahead, and you brace yourself. The moment the cab stops you will open the door and run off. The cab slows, then stops. You reach for the door handle. Then you realize that there is no door handle!

In a panic you look at the other door. There isn't a handle over there either. The driver pulls out a revolver. It's too dangerous to try to escape.

You have no idea where you are headed, and nobody knows where you are. You hope the police can trace your bicycle...before it's too late.

THE END

from page 47

According to the directory of the building overlooking the park, two people share the sixteenth floor: L. Jasper, 16A, and W. Rush, 16B. But the man you followed could be anyone. You must find out first if he is Jasper or Rush. If you could find that out, you might have a talk with Lieutenant Duffy. But how to find out?

You decide to pretend to be a delivery boy and to visit both apartments. You buy two boxes of flowers at a flower shop down the street, and in a few moments you are in the lobby of the building.

"Flower deliveries for Jasper and Rush," you tell the man at the desk.

He nods, and you go to the elevator. You get off at sixteen and ring the bell on the left, 16A. A card on the door reads L. JASPER. A woman answers.

"Flowers," you say, handing her the box.

"Oh, how lovely," she says. "He remembered my birthday."

You give her a smile. When she closes the door, you cross the hall and ring the other bell, W. RUSH, 16B.

"Flowers," you say to the man who opens the door.

You recognize him. He is the man who was watching you and Peter. He was the man you followed. As you pass him the box of flowers, you turn your head slightly, so he can't get a good look at your face.

"That's nice of you," the man says. "Say, listen, you must know something about flowers."

"Yes, sir," you say.

"Come with me," he says. "I need your help with something."

Not wanting to make him suspicious, you follow him through the apartment to the terrace outside. It is huge, and in one corner is a small tool shed.

"Let me show you what's the matter," he says, opening the door to the tool shed.

You look inside. Then you feel a hand on your shoulder, and you are shoved inside the shed. The door closes behind you, and you hear a lock snap shut.

He recognized you! And now you are trapped.

THE END

from page 34/from page 37

At the county clerk's office, a search of the records shows the owner of the Dixie Warehouse to be a man living in a nearby city. This doesn't tell you much. But like a thorough detective, you show the clerk your drawing of the strange ring. No luck. The clerk shakes his head.

Then a man from the next office walks by. He is from the Department of Public Works, and he immediately reacts to your drawing.

"Why, just the other day someone was in with a ring like that," he says, "looking at maps."

"What kind of maps?" you ask.

"Maps showing the tunnels for electric cables," he says.

When you ask for more information, the man explains that beneath the streets of your town are tunnels carrying electric cables to office buildings and homes. The cables may share these tunnels with sewer pipes, oil pipes, and underground telephone wires. Maps of these tunnels are kept in the county office building, and a building contractor, for example, would consult these maps before constructing a building.

"What part of the city did these maps show?" you ask.

"Over near the park," he says.

"Including the museum?"

"Including the museum."

Now, *that* is interesting. After looking over the same tunnel maps, you call the information desk at the museum and ask what the latest exhibit is. The voice at the other end informs you that it is an exhibit on ancient Egypt, featuring the famous bust of Ha-tep.

That's it! The criminals must be planning to steal the bust from the museum! That must be the head the men in Tiny's store were talking about. You assume that they will simply leave the marathon race near the museum, enter the building, steal the head, and try to escape unnoticed within a large pack of marathon runners. They probably plan to hide the head in the backpack they bought at Tiny's store. And now you have a good idea of how they plan to enter the museum: from a tunnel.

Should you visit the tunnel alone to find out how and where they plan to enter the museum? If you knew that, you could alert the police. Or should you get your big friend Tiny to go with you?

If you think you should visit the tunnel alone, turn to page 66.

If you think you should ask Tiny to join you, turn to page 69.

from page 31

From covering last year's race, you know that Sanders and Fennimore belong to the same track club. That club works out at the 23rd Street track. That may be the best place to look for them.

When you get there, you ask an attendant if Sanders or Fennimore has checked in today.

"Sanders isn't here today. We haven't seen him all day," says the attendant. "But Fennimore is out on the track right now, warming up for tomorrow."

You ask the attendant to point Fennimore out to you. Then you approach the runner as he leisurely jogs around the track.

"Excuse me," you say in a tone of authority, jogging along beside him, "I'm doing a story on the marathon race and need some background. You are Mr. Fennimore, aren't you?"

"Yes, I am," he replies.

"I know you came in second last year," you say, "but I don't remember who came in third. I thought perhaps you would know."

"To tell you the truth," Fennimore says, "I don't recall. I was so tired at the end of the race and so glad to finish that I didn't pay much attention to who came in after me."

"Do you know where Mr. Sanders is?" you ask. You figure you should play dumb. "He was last year's winner, wasn't he?" you add.

"That's right. But would you believe this? Karl sprained his ankle pretty badly in training yesterday. It doesn't look like he'll be able to race tomorrow."

"Oh, that's too bad," you say.

Wanting to confirm Fennimore's story, you ask the attendant to point out the trainer for the facility. When you catch up with the trainer, he verifies the fact that Sanders sprained his ankle badly yesterday and was advised to stay off of it for at least a week. You thank the trainer for his help and head back outside.

Well, that does it, you think. Sanders and Fennimore can't have anything to do with kidnapping Peter Andrews. They have no motive. Fennimore doesn't even remember Andrews, and Sanders is out of the race.

All you can do is try to pursue another lead. You decide to go back to Tiny's store and have a talk with him about the two men you overheard in his store.

Turn to page 10.

from page 121

When you arrive at Tiny's sports shop, he is preparing to close the store for the evening. As he rings out the cash register, you explain about the uncle, the phone calls, and how he could hear what sounded like a train in the background.

"A train," says Tiny. "There aren't many trains around town anymore, are there?"

"A few big freight trains still go through town," you say. "But there are not many of those."

"And the electric train," Tiny says. "The old one that still runs out to Millburn."

You and Tiny call the railroad office in town. You learn from a freight dispatcher that no freight train has passed through town since late Friday night. Tiny has a car, so the two of you drive to the office of the electric railway. Here, you look over the schedules. After a while, the two of you are able to pinpoint a place on a map—a place where the 2:30 P.M. train could have passed at 2:45, and a 9:50 A.M. train could have passed that morning at 10:10. The place on the map is to the west of town. According to the map, the area does not seem to be heavily built up. You do know, from having lived in your town all your life, that there is not much out there other than a few run-down old buildings. The two of you decide to drive out there.

When you arrive, you can plainly see that there is only one building near the electric railroad track. The others are too far away from the line to be likely candidates.

As soon as you get close enough to the building, you both realize it is a perfect place to have hidden Peter. The place is a sanatorium, a brick building with bars on the windows. It is something like a hospital but built so people inside can't get out. It is also fairly isolated. It stands all alone on the block, with only a gas station across the street. As you sit in Tiny's car, you notice a laundry truck parked in front of the sanatorium.

As you watch, the driver leaves the truck. But instead of going into the sanatorium, he walks across the street into the gas station, probably to grab a quick soda before his rounds. This may be your best opportunity.

"Are you thinking what I'm thinking?" you say to Tiny.

"Yes," he answers. "Let's go."

You open the back of the truck, and each of you takes a bundle of clean laundry. You walk up to the front door and ring the bell.

"Laundry," Tiny says to the white-uniformed man who answers the door.

"Down the hall," the man says. "The storage room on the right."

As you walk down the hall, both of you look around. Most of the people you see are dressed in white uniforms. They are big, tough-looking men, but they pay little attention to you. At the storage room you keep right on going. You see a staircase, and you both start walking up. On the second floor you pause on the landing. Down at the end of the hall, near the back of the building, you spot a man in a dark suit. He opens a door and goes inside a room. You and Tiny look at each other, then walk down the hall. You stop outside the door. Inside you can hear voices. Tiny knocks on the door, and the man in the suit opens the door.

"Laundry," Tiny says.

"This isn't the storage room," the man snaps.

"Hold this, would you?" Tiny says, passing him the laundry. Instinctively, the man reaches out. Tiny drops the laundry and grabs the man. Through the wide-open door, you see Peter Andrews tied to a chair. He has a surprised look on his face.

The good news is that you have found Peter.

The bad news is that the men in white uniforms are all over the place. Someone will see you if you try to escape.

Tiny turns the man in the suit around and places a huge hand over his mouth. You step into the room, looking around for a telephone. You start untying Peter from the chair.

"Am I glad to see you!" Peter says.

"Peter, where's the phone you used when you spoke to your uncle?"

"In the next room," says Peter.

"Is there somebody in there?" you ask.

"I don't think so."

"We could phone for the police," Tiny says.

"We're out in the middle of nowhere," you say.

"It'll take them too long to arrive," says Peter.

"Or we could make a run for it," Tiny says.

"And fight our way through those guys in the white uniforms?" you say.

"Either way," Peter says, "they're sure to realize what's happening sooner or later. Probably sooner."

If you think you should phone for the police, turn to page 64.

If you think you should make a run for it, turn to page 68.

from page 121

Deciding to act alone, you jump onto your bicycle and head for the railroad office.

When you arrive, you take one of the local-train schedules and read the arrivals column carefully. You see that a train stops down near the river on the west side of town at 10:10 A.M. and at 2:45 P.M. You decide to take a little ride to the other side of town.

You follow the train tracks from the station, riding carefully next to the rail line.

After riding for an hour, you begin to feel tired. You're not looking where you are going, and without realizing it, you drive your front tire over a broken bottle lying near the railroad track. The tire collapses and you have to get off and walk.

You can't just leave your bike here, so you decide to walk it home and leave it there until it can be taken care of. By the time you get home, it will probably be too late to solve the mystery.

THE END

from page 62

You decide to call the police. Because the sanatorium is far from town, it takes a while for them to get to you. But once they arrive, they rush to where you are on the second floor, over the objections of the men in white. Soon, you and Tiny and Peter are telling Lieutenant Duffy the whole story. The man in the suit confesses, and the police fan out to pick up the others in the kidnap gang.

Now a big part of the mystery is revealed. The threat against Peter—that he'd be in danger if he ran the race—was a "red herring," or false clue. The kidnappers made Peter withdraw from the race to cast suspicion on others in the marathon. The fact that he worked at the museum also meant nothing in this case.

Peter's uncle is a rich businessman and has enough money to pay the criminals a healthy ransom. The criminals threatened Peter so that when the gang kidnapped him, if Peter's uncle did go to the police, everybody would think the kidnapping had something to do with the marathon race. This could throw the police off the track. The kidnapping was a classic, old-fashioned one. It had to do with getting a big ransom.

The next day, Peter does run in the race. And he comes in second, even though the kidnapping experience was upsetting.

You congratulate Peter at the finish line. He has done extremely well under the circumstances.

"Next year," he tells you, "I *will* come in first."

Later in the day you find out from Lieutenant Duffy that the two men in Tiny's store *were* planning a crime on the day of the marathon race. They tried to steal the priceless bust of Egypt's ancient queen Ha-tep from the traveling exhibit now on display in your town's museum. But the museum had doubled security for this special exhibit, and the criminals were caught in the act.

You are glad the criminals were caught, and you are proud that you solved your own marathon-race mystery.

THE END

from page 55

You decide to visit the tunnel on your own. But first you go to the Department of Public Works and explain to an official that you are a reporter for your school newspaper. You say that your readers would be interested in what goes on underneath your town. The official is glad to make some arrangements for you.

A municipal worker accompanies you to a manhole cover near the museum, and both of you climb down a ladder into the tunnel. No sooner are you in the tunnel than the city worker responds to a beep on his paging machine. He is needed for an emergency, he tells you. "Stay where you are," he suggests. "I'll be back soon."

Now you are alone with a map and a flashlight. You hear some kind of scraping noise ahead. Cautiously, you move forward. The noise becomes louder. You turn off the flashlight.

"That about does it," you hear a voice say.

"One good push and we're through," says another.

Ahead of you are two men. Their flashlight plays on a metal door. The men are doing something to the lock.

"We'll leave it this way until tomorrow morning," one of them says.

The flashlight's beam leaves the door, shines for a second on the ceiling of the tunnel, and then, before you can move, swings your way. Desperately, you hug the tunnel wall.

"What the—?" one of the man says, seeing you.

Turning your flashlight on, you run away as fast as you can. Behind you comes the sound of pounding feet. At first you hold your own, keeping about the same distance from the two men. But soon they are gaining on you.

The tunnel does not look familiar anymore, and you wonder if you took a wrong turn. Ahead you see two doors. The one on the left is marked STORAGE, the one on the right DANGER: DO NOT ENTER. The men are almost upon you.

If you want to take the door on the right, turn to page 91.

If you want to take the door on the left, turn to page 92.

from page 62

There's no time to wait for the police. You quickly tie up and gag the man in the suit. The windows are barred, so the only way you can leave is the same way you came in. But how? If you take Peter, you won't be out in the hall for more than a minute before you're noticed. Time for a quick decision. You decide the only way out is to make a run for it and hope for the best.

The three of you take a deep breath, then open the door and start running. In a matter of seconds, bells are ringing and the men in white coats are after you. Even with Tiny on your side, you have to give up. There are too many of them, and three of the men have guns. Guns are one thing even Tiny can't fight. The men take the three of you back to the room where they were holding Peter and tie you to chairs.

The kidnapping plot proceeds on schedule. Peter's uncle delivers the ransom money.

Unfortunately, the kidnappers cannot let you go. The three of you know too much. Before the gang takes off with the ransom, they move you, Tiny, and Peter to the basement, behind a stack of old boxes. By the time you're found, the thieves will be long gone. And whatever those two men in Tiny's store were up to, someone else will have to stop them. For your investigation, this is . . .

THE END

from page 55

You call Tiny and ask him to check out the tunnels beneath the museum with you. After all, if the crooks are snooping around down there, figuring out how to get into the museum without being seen, you'll need your big friend.

You remember that before Tiny opened his sporting-goods store, he had worked briefly for the Department of Public Works. The department official will let you and Tiny visit the tunnels without an escort.

Later in the afternoon, Tiny meets you at the manhole cover near the museum. Tiny knows how to read the map of the tunnel system, and soon you are both heading through the tunnels toward the museum.

"We're under the building now," Tiny says.

Suddenly you both hear a noise ahead. Tiny puts a finger to his lips, and together you quietly move forward. The noise becomes a little louder—a scraping sound, like that of metal on metal. It appears that somewhere ahead the criminals are tampering with a lock.

You and Tiny turn off your flashlights and move forward ever so slowly.

"That about does it," you hear a voice say.

"One good push and we're through," says another.

Ahead of you, you can see the beam of a flashlight playing on a metal door. The men are obviously finishing up their business with the museum's basement-door lock.

"We'll leave it this way until tomorrow morning," one of them says.

You see the flashlight beam leave the door and shine for a second on the ceiling of the tunnel. Then, before you and Tiny can move, the light beam swings in your direction. You and Tiny hug the wall. But the light has found you.

"Who the—?" says one of the men.

"Get them!" cries the other.

You and Tiny turn and run. For a big man, Tiny is fast, and you do pretty well yourself. But the men behind you must be faster, because their footsteps are pounding nearer and nearer.

"They're going to catch us," you yell to Tiny.

"When I say stop, stop and turn around," Tiny says.

In a few more moments, Tiny says, "Stop!"

Turning around, you notice that the men are nearly on top of you, and you thank your lucky stars that Tiny is with you. Tiny grabs the men, and the three of them rock this way and that. You grab at one of the men and succeed in pulling him away. Then Tiny, swinging a big fist, catches the other man on the jaw, and he collides with your man.

You and Tiny are both off balance. As you get set to resume the fight, the two men turn and race away down the tunnel. The two of you listen to the sounds of footsteps echoing down the tunnel. Soon it is quiet again.

"Sorry they got away," you say to Tiny.

"That's all right," Tiny says. "At least we know how they plan to get into the museum."

Your mind races back to the matter at hand. Three options occur to you. Your first option is to go to the finish line and wait for the crooks to complete the race. You may be able to catch them red-handed.

Your second option is to phone the police and tell them that you and Tiny saw the soon-to-be criminals rigging the museum door for their robbery scheme.

Your final option is to try to second-guess the crooks. Not only did you and Tiny give them a real scare; they also saw you and Tiny witnessing their work in the electrical tunnel. Will they follow through with their plan now? Or will they try some other scheme, using a different entrance to the Ha-tep exhibit? Perhaps you should poke around for another entrance the thieves might use to enter the museum.

If you think you can wrap up this case by waiting at the finish line of the marathon, turn to page 100.

If you want to talk to the police, turn to page 93.

If you want to try to find another way into the museum, turn to page 8.

from page 44

You talk to Lieutenant Duffy at police headquarters and carefully explain everything you've discovered.

The lieutenant listens patiently, then shakes his head. "I appreciate your coming to see me, but I need more solid evidence. If you find out more, let me know, but I can't do anything now. Besides, we already have an officer guarding the bust around the clock. Thanks for coming in, though."

When you leave the police station, it is getting dark outside. Fall leaves are scattering over the pavement, pushed by the October wind. You ride your bike back through the park to the museum. As you ride, you have a feeling that you are being followed. You turn around, but in the gloom you cannot be sure. Several times you think you see a vehicle behind you, traveling without lights.

You cut across the park on a wide bicycle path. From time to time, overhead lights shine down on the path. Again, you have the feeling that you're being followed. Finally, as you enter a tunnel passing under a major park road, you suddenly hear the roar of an engine thundering behind you.

The van savagely forces your bike off the road. If you hadn't moved quickly, you might have been killed.

As the van screeches away, and you pick up your bike, you decide that this is where your investigation will end. It's just too dangerous. You'll call the police and tell them what you know. They can handle it from here.

THE END

from page 44

The television station in your town is located in the newspaper building. Your TV news friend, Arthur Manning, meets you in his office. Together you study a map on the wall of his office. You explain what you suspect about the head, and that you think it may be stolen during the marathon race.

"Before and during the race, we can't be everywhere," you say, "but your cameras can help."

"What's your idea?" Manning asks.

"Since the race is tomorrow, lots of the runners have been doing last-minute warmup exercises. I think the men who are after the head have been out there, too. If I'm right, the crooks want to know every inch of the course that goes near the museum. What kind of pre-race coverage has your station been broadcasting?"

"We've had camera crews out all week," Manning says. "We've shown runners training and done interviews with contestants and officials."

"Do you keep your old video footage on file?"

"Yes, we do," says Manning. "We keep it for a few weeks."

You ask if you can view the station's videotape file. Arthur is not completely convinced that you are onto something, but he's willing to go along with the idea.

"I guess it could be a big story," he says, "for you *and* for us."

You watch the footage taken that day as Arthur explains his station's procedures. Many reporters and camera crews are sent out each day to cover stories all over town. From the reels of tape brought in by the crews, short segments of each are selected for the day's newscast while the rest is set aside to be filed or discarded. During the screening of today's tape, something catches your attention.

A camera crew had taken shots of runners training a few miles back from the finish line. During the taping, the camera panned over to the nearby parking lot. For a brief moment you see a van with two men standing behind it. Did you see pyramids on the side? And were the men wearing long white coats?

"Can you back that up," you ask, "and freeze on that van and the two men?"

The technician backs up the film and holds the picture motionless in what is called a "freeze frame." Sure enough, there *are* pyramids on the side of the van. But this van has no license plate in the front. Could there be more than one pyramid van? One of the men has his back toward you. From the two words written on the back of his white coat you can read only two

letters. The first letter of the first word is D, and the second letter of the second word is A.

You look in the telephone book under D for a two-word listing matching this combination. Then you write down the two letters you can read, with blanks for letters you can't read. Finally you write down some possible answers from the phone book:

D _ _ _ _	_ A _ _ _ _ _ _ _ _
D O N U T	B A K E S H O P S
D I A N A	B A R B E R H U T
D I X I E	W A R E H O U S E
D O U G 'S	L A N D F I L L S
D E A N 'S	D A I R Y L A N D

You ask the technician to roll the tape back one more time. Upon closer inspection, you can see that the last letter of the second word is either a D or an E. That narrows your options.

If you think you should check out the Dixie Warehouse, turn to page 35.

If you think you should check out Dean's Dairyland, turn to page 80.

from page 79

Dean's Dairyland turns out to be a modest ice-cream shop on the other side of town. You have never been there before. When you get there, you order a cone of "Georgia peach" ice cream. This will give you more time to linger and observe.

As you enjoy your cone, you witness several ice-cream purchases, all apparently normal. Then something happens that catches your attention. The young man who has attracted your attention is a nervous type. He keeps shifting his weight from one foot to the other. He has ordered a "Cairo cream" cone. Since Cairo is the capital of Egypt, you believe this could be some kind of signal. As the woman behind the counter dishes out two scoops, you notice for the briefest moment a quick movement of the man's hand. Did he insert a small piece of paper inside his ice cream?

You finish your cone and quietly follow the nervous young man out of Dean's Dairyland. Outside, on the street, you follow him as he walks along.

Still showing nervousness, the young man works his way through his ice-cream cone. There is no sign of his encountering a hidden piece of paper. Finally he downs the rest of the cone. Then, still shifting from foot to foot and appearing ill at ease, he pauses in front of a door. All at once, he enters the building. On the door is a lettered sign.

DR. YOUNG. DENTIST.

So much for Cairo cream, you think to yourself. It was only a coincidence that put you on a false lead.

Even the best detectives sometimes need outside help. Whom should you ask?

If you think you should go ask Tiny for ideas and help, turn to page 82.

If you think you should go to the police, turn to page 84.

from page 81

You go to Tiny's store to discuss your strategy. Your story gives Tiny an idea.

"You've gone a long way towards solving this case," he says. "Now you should have two goals. One is to make sure the crooks don't steal the head. The other is to see that they're arrested. There's only one problem. To get them arrested, you'll have to let them steal the head. All you have now is a theory. But if you first let them steal the head and then catch them, then you have proof."

"Maybe I can get my friend Arthur Manning, the TV reporter, to put a camera outside the museum and film them in the act," you say.

"Or there's an even better idea . . ." Tiny begins.

"You mean put the camera inside the gallery and get a shot of whoever breaks into the case and takes the head?" you ask.

"I do. That would make the evening news all over America."

"But these men are criminals," you say to your friend. "Without the help of the police, we could all be in danger."

If you think you should go back to see Arthur Manning, turn to page 87.

If you would rather go to the police, turn to page 84.

from page 14

The line at the Department of Motor Vehicles is at least twenty people long. You stand in line for forty-five minutes before you reach the desk.

"Can I help you?" the clerk behind the counter asks.

"Yes, I want to trace the license-plate number on a vehicle, to find out who owns it," you say.

"I'm sorry, we can't do that for unauthorized personnel," the clerk answers.

Thinking fast, you tell them that a van almost knocked you off your bicycle and that you would like to find out which business or company the van belongs to. You try your best to look sincere.

"Well, I'm sorry, but an incident of that nature is something for the police to handle."

"But I—"

You are cut off by the clerk.

"I'm sorry I can't help you," the clerk says. "Have a nice day. Next, please."

Well, it was a long shot. You realize your time would have been better spent at the museum. You quickly pedal back to the museum before it closes in an hour.

Turn to page 42.

from page 81/from page 82

Lieutenant Duffy of your town's police department is a busy man. You quickly review for him everything you've learned—the ring, the overheard conversation, the museum, and the head of Ha-tep.

"You may be onto something," he tells you. "But I really don't have the time to look into this myself, and I can't spare any of my men. I will alert the museum, though, and have them see that the guard there stays alert. Thanks for coming in."

You are disappointed by Lieutenant Duffy's response. Now there is only one thing you can do: call Arthur Manning. With his cooperation you may be able to obtain the proof you need to put the crooks away, and to save the bust at the same time.

On the other hand, you could wait at the finish line of the race and let the thieves come to you.

If you want to see Arthur Manning, turn to page 87.

If you want to wait at the finish line, turn to page 90.

from page 37

The county clerk could have told you who owns the property, but a real-estate agent can tell you more. He or she will also know if anyone is trying to buy or sell the place. And this could supply you with a clue as to what is going on at the warehouse.

Your real-estate friend is a nice man whom you know from your own neighborhood. He tells you that the warehouse is owned by a man in a nearby city. There's not much significance in that. Your friend does know, however, that another man is interested in buying the warehouse and that he has made several trips there to look over the place.

"What is his name?" you ask.

Your friend consults his notebook, then writes down a name and address on a piece of paper: MR. IMIR. 420 HILLTOP DRIVE.

"You mean the *haunted* house?" you ask.

"The old Beatty house," he says. "I know you may have heard it's haunted, but it's really just an old house, even if the Beatty family was murdered there years ago."

"Is Mr. Imir renting the house?" you ask.

"For a month. He's also in town to run in the marathon. He says that he's been training on the marathon route almost every day."

You show your friend the drawing of the ring.

"Have you ever seen this?" you ask.

"Why, yes. Mr. Imir wears a ring with that design."

"What does he look like?" you ask.

"He's a big man. Very big, with dark hair and a scar on his cheek."

You feel you have two choices, and each one may be dangerous. You can visit the Beatty house and see what Mr. Imir is up to or you can hang around the race course and hope to keep an eye on Mr. Imir as he warms up for the marathon.

If you think you should visit the Beatty house, turn to page 97.

If you think you should hang around the race course, turn to page 94.

from page 82/from page 84

You decide to go back to see Arthur Manning. There is no more dramatic scoop for a TV reporter than to videotape a crime in progress. If the crime is big enough, the tape of it will make the evening news all across the country. Your proposal works. Arthur's network agrees to hide a videotape camera and an operator inside the gallery.

On Sunday morning, the day of the race, you take your position with Arthur in the TV booth at the finish line. In front of you is a bank of TV monitors, displaying pictures of the race course from various locations. But one camera is focused on a glass case with a golden bust inside.

At about the time that most of the lead runners have already passed behind the museum, you suddenly notice in the museum monitor two runners, one dressed in combat uniform, approaching the glass case. But where is the guard? Has something gone wrong?

Staring at the monitor, you see the men break open the case, take the bust, then leave the range of the camera. Now all they have to do is pose as runners and finish the race. No one will suspect a thing—except you.

265

You have to act fast. Soon the lead runner appears down the road, heading for the finish line. Lieutenant Duffy is standing nearby.

"Lieutenant, I have an important videotape to show you," you say. "And I think you should send a radio car up to the museum. In the meantime, keep your eyes on the race. In particular, be on the lookout for two men running together. One of the men will have a heavy object in his backpack.

"I think I see them now, Lieutenant. You may wish to have a few words with them."

The criminals are swiftly captured. At the museum, Lieutenant Duffy's officers find the security guard assigned to protect the bust. The criminals had overpowered him and locked him in a utility closet.

You have solved the marathon-race mystery.

THE END

from page 84

Although Lieutenant Duffy can't help you, you know you can wrap up this case. The next morning, the day of the race, Lieutenant Duffy stands at the finish line with some of his officers. Suddenly, the lead runner appears in the distance. The crowd begins cheering.

You go over to Lieutenant Duffy and whisper a few words to him. He gives you a funny look, as if he doesn't believe you. Soon the runners begin pounding across the finish line.

A few moments later, you see the two men. One, as you expected, has a large object in his backpack. When he is almost opposite you, you leave the crowd. The next moment, you sprint and lock your arms around the man.

The crowd yells in anger. Looking up, you see the police surround you and the two runners. They arrest the man with the strange ring. He holds on to the backpack as if he isn't going to give it up.

You gently take the golden bust from him. You've caught the thieves red-handed and solved the marathon-race mystery.

THE END

from page 67

You run to the door on the right and grasp the knob. The knob does not move! This door is locked!

The men grab you from behind.

"Let's open the door for the kid," one says to the other. "Where are those keys we stole?" They shove you inside a dark, musty room and lock the door behind you.

You hope that your friend from the Department of Public Works will find you quickly. Otherwise, you could be down here for a long time.

THE END

from page 67

You choose the door on the left. You're in luck! You open the unlocked door and enter the basement of the museum. But the men are still after you. Desperately you run, but in your haste your foot hits something on the floor, and you trip. The next thing you know you are lying on the floor and the men are standing over you.

"It's a little squirt," one of the men says.

"Yeah, kind of small," the other says. "Like one of those ancient Egyptians. I think that mummy case over there would be a perfect spot for our new pal."

You never should have gone into the tunnel alone, you realize. If only you'd taken Tiny along.

You feel a hand reaching out for you, and you smell an unpleasant odor. Chloroform. In a moment you'll be unconscious.

You hope you wake up before the man from the Department of Public Works comes in here looking for you. He'll never look in the mummy case unless he hears a lot of noise from inside.

THE END

from page 73

You and Tiny convince the police that a museum robbery is planned for tomorrow's marathon. You both have bruises from your encounter in the tunnel, and Lieutenant Duffy is further convinced when he inspects the underground door to the museum and notices that the lock has been tampered with.

It is a simple matter to arrange a stake-out in the museum. However, the crooks aren't that stupid. They know you saw what they were planning. The robbery never takes place and the thieves go uncaught and unpunished.

THE END

from page 86

On any day before the marathon race, dozens of runners may be found training on the course. They do not run the entire twenty-six-mile course, but those who live nearby run parts of it during the weeks before the race.

During their training sessions, many runners cover most of the actual course. In this way a runner becomes familiar with every hill, and every twist and turn.

You ride your bike to the finish line of the race and then in the direction of the starting line. This way the runners will be jogging in the opposite direction—toward you. With any luck, you may be able to spot Mr. Imir. But you don't have much to go on. You are looking for a big man with dark hair, a scar on his cheek, and, of course, the ring, if you can get close enough to see that.

As you ride, you pass several tall, heavyset runners with dark hair. Each time, you turn your bike and follow the runner. Each time you get close enough, you see that none of these men is wearing the strange ring. None has a scarred cheek.

Not far from the starting line you see another large, dark-haired man. Once again, you turn your bike around. Now you get lucky. Riding behind him, you are fairly certain that he has a ring on his left hand. And although he moves his hand back and forth as he runs, his ring appears to be the one you're looking for. You can't be sure, but he may also have a scar on his right cheek.

To make certain, you ride close behind him and lean forward over the handlebars. You are so intent on catching a glimpse of the ring that you fail to see a pothole in the road. The next thing you know, your bike is out of control and both you and your bike hit the big man.

"You stupid kid!" the big man says.

"I'm sorry, Mr. Imir. I'm terribly sorry."

"How do you know my name?"

Then you notice the ring on his hand—the same ring with the strange design you saw on the man in Tiny's shop. Mr. Imir's eyes are narrowed in anger. When he talks, he makes a sort of hissing sound.

"How do you know my name?" he repeats.

"Uh, from, from . . . the race office," you say, thinking fast. "I was there when you registered for the marathon. I just remember you, that's all."

He stares at you for a long time. Although other runners are passing you, and it is a sunny October day, you feel as though it is the middle of the night and you are all alone in the world with Mr. Imir.

"I'm sorry, Mr. Imir," you repeat. "I'll be more careful in the future."

He gives you a sour look, then turns around and resumes his running, trying to get back his stride. At this point it would be dangerous to follow him. But if you did follow him, you might be able to find out more about what he's planning to do. Or would it be better to follow him during the race itself?

If you think you should follow Mr. Imir now, turn to page 101.

If you think you should follow him on your bike during the race, turn to page 104.

from page 86

You don't really believe in haunted houses. After all, a house is just a house, even if it is empty and falling apart, and even if an entire family was once murdered there. Still, you'd better think this through clearly.

You realize, for example, that there is no point in visiting the house at night. It will be too dark to see anything. So you'll go during the day. Should you bring friends with you? Would ten or twenty of them be enough? Don't be ridiculous. It's just an old house.

As you park your bike against the rusty iron fence that surrounds the Beatty house, the sun goes behind a cloud. It becomes quite dark outside. The wind seems to pick up. A loose shutter bangs back and forth. You button up your jacket and start up the driveway.

Maybe you *should* have some friends with you, you think, walking up the weed-clogged driveway. The place appears to be completely deserted. Why would Mr. Imir rent such a place?

You walk up the steps to the front door. One of the steps is loose, and the wood groans under your foot.

On the front porch, you try looking through a window, but the dark drapes inside block your view. You put your ear to the front door, listening for a sound. Was that a board creaking on the other side? Suddenly, you realize that your ear is no longer pressed against the door. The door is open.

Towering over you is a giant of a man. You notice the familiar ring on his right hand and the scar on his cheek. It can be only Mr. Imir.

If you think you should tell Mr. Imir that you are looking for a lost pet, turn to page 110.

If you think you should try to make a run for it, turn to page 113.

from page 73

The next day, surrounded by the excitement of the marathon race, you wait at the finish line for the runners to pass, including, you are certain, the two men who will steal the head of Ha-tep.

The first runners cross the finish line. Many others cross the finish line as you wait there in the October sunshine for the men with the bust. As time passes, several hundred runners finish the race. More time goes by, and finally the last weary athletes cross the line. And the crooks still have not appeared.

Then you realize why.

You had caught the thieves in the act of preparing the museum door. The thieves know that you spotted them. What intelligent crooks would commit a crime that someone had solved ahead of time?

The head of Ha-tep is safe. There has been no robbery; you have prevented that. But the would-be robbers have made good their escape. You will not catch them, and they may try again another day.

You'd better get busy on your story about the marathon. There is not much news in a robbery that didn't take place.

THE END

from page 96

Following Mr. Imir is a bold step, and it might be dangerous. But it may be the best way to discover his plans.

This time, you stay far behind Mr. Imir. Several times he turns to see if he is being followed, but you are quite certain that he does not notice you.

Approaching the rear of your town's museum, the big man pauses, and you stop riding. He seems to be checking out the back of the building. Then he walks around the museum to a parking lot in front. As you watch, he walks over to a parked red van and begins talking to the driver. The van has pyramids painted on the side.

Now you have a problem. If the two drive off in the van, you will surely lose them. You can't keep up on your bike.

You decide to take a chance. As the men stand there talking, you ride around to the other side of the museum and lock your bike on a bike rack. When the men get into the van, you hail a taxi. Now that you have such a strong lead, you feel you must pursue it.

"Follow that van," you tell the driver.

You follow the van into the warehouse and freight district down by the waterfront. You are not surprised to see the van pull up in front of the Dixie Warehouse. You pay the driver and approach the warehouse on foot. You are careful to stay on the other side of the street, out of sight of anyone else who might be approaching the warehouse. Soon other men arrive. They park their cars in the empty parking lot and enter the old building by the front door.

After a while it seems that no one else will be arriving. You decide to take the biggest chance so far—to enter the building through the front door. You quietly slip inside the door and enter a big room filled with crates and boxes. In the middle of the room, a meeting is in progress. Mr. Imir seems to be in charge.

"Tomorrow is the marathon race," he says. "And you all know the plan. I don't want any mistakes. Any questions?"

The group around him is silent.

"All right, Milo," Mr. Imir says, turning to a man near him. "You take the van to Smith's Garage. They have all the painting equipment there. Then you drive the van to the first-aid tent tomorrow. You know what to do from there."

Apparently the men plan to change the look of their van. But what will they change it into? And why are they going to meet at the marathon's first-aid tent?

If you think you should continue to watch Mr. Imir, turn to page 117.

If you think you should go directly to Smith's Garage, turn to page 106.

from page 96

It won't be easy to follow Mr. Imir during the marathon race. There are more than five thousand runners in the race. Finding Mr. Imir, and then staying behind him, could be a real job. But you do know one important thing. Mr. Imir and his friend plan to take the head from the museum and escape among the runners. But will he start the race at the beginning, leave it near the museum, take the head, and rejoin the race? That way he would call attention to himself twice—once by leaving the race and again by getting back into it.

Or will Mr. Imir enter the museum in some way and then join the race with the head in his backpack? If so, you would be smart to wait near the museum and follow him from there. But even this could be a problem. There would still be dozens of runners passing near the museum at a time, and spotting him could be difficult. Also, you do not know the racing number that he'll have to wear on his uniform. Your real-estate friend told you that Mr. Imir was trying to buy the warehouse, but you haven't had time to check that name with the race officials.

On the day of the race, you decide to wait at the starting line. But as you had feared, you never see the man you want to follow. The racers crossing the line are thirty or forty deep where you stand.

Your investigation is over. All you can do now is cover the rest of the race. After all, you promised your editor a story about the marathon.

THE END

from page 103/from page 117

Smith's Garage is located on the waterfront. The business has a poor reputation. Its owner, Bill Smith, is a man often in trouble with the law, Smith's Garage is definitely the kind of place where a stolen vehicle could be expertly painted and altered. It could be done quietly here, with no questions asked.

When you arrive at Smith's Garage, Milo and the van are already there. They soon disappear inside the shop. You figure it may take all night before the "new" van reappears. You take a taxi home and and try to get a good night's sleep. You'll need all your energy tomorrow.

Early the next morning, you return to the waterfront and wait for the van to reappear. In half an hour, a brightly painted vehicle emerges. The pyramids are now gone and the red color has been changed to white. Letters spelling AMBULANCE appear on the front of the van, and a red cross is painted on the side. But you also notice something that convinces you these men may not be so smart after all. It's the way

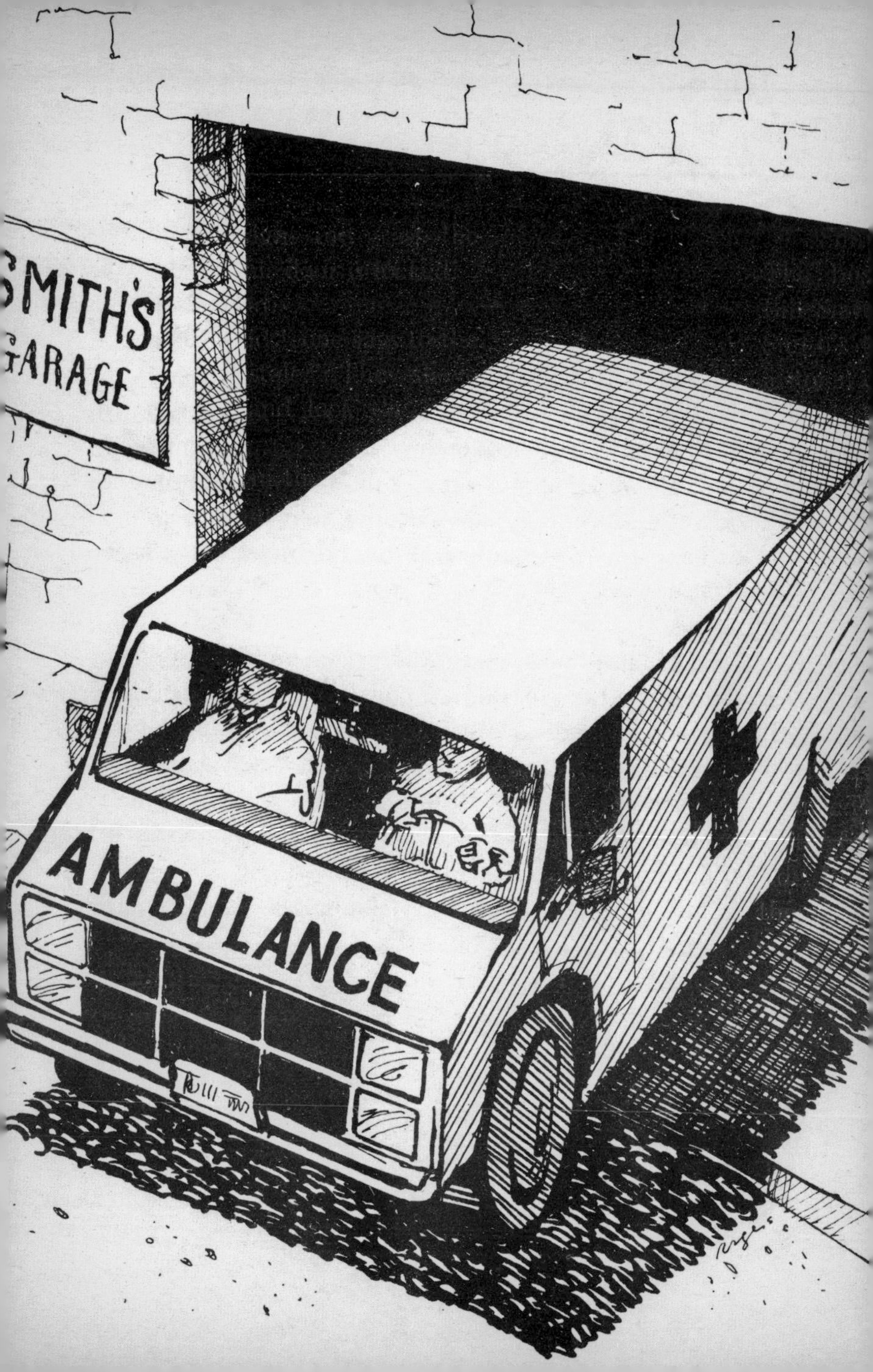
SMITH'S
GARAGE
AMBULANCE

they painted the ambulance: they forgot one important detail. They painted the word "ambulance" from left to right, so it can be read just by looking at it. They forgot that most new ambulances have the word "ambulance" painted backward on the front, so any driver looking in his or her rearview mirror can read it. This mistake will make the "ambulance" a cinch to spot. If your hunch is right, the same ambulance will be at the finish line in a matter of hours. You hop in a cab and spend your last four dollars to get to the race course.

A marathon race can be very demanding on the human body. First-aid stations care for any runner who needs medical assistance. Near the finish line of many marathon races are medical tents. Here nurses and doctors attend to those who have pushed their bodies a little too far. Several ambulances stand by to transport serious cases to the hospital.

You recognize the phony ambulance in a second.

When you manage to touch it on one side without being noticed, white paint comes off on your hand. Milo, you notice, is standing apart from the vehicle, dressed in the white uniform of an ambulance attendant.

Now what should you do? To get the Ha-tep bust, these men will probably set up some diversion at the museum to get the guard away from the exhibit. Mr. Imir and the other man, dressed in fatigues and back-packs, will take the head and join the crowd of marathon runners. Near the finish line, they will pretend to have some sort of injury and make their final escape in the ambulance.

If you think you should contact the police, turn to page 114.

If you think you should get Tiny to help you foil the robbery, turn to page 111.

If you think you should handle this alone, turn to page 116.

from page 99

As the man's giant hand reaches for you, you hope your explanation about the lost pet will sound convincing. After all, pets are lost all the time.

"I . . . I was looking for . . . Have you seen a little white poodle?' you say.

"Let's look in the basement," the man says, grabbing you by the collar and pulling you inside. He pushes you down the stairway and locks the door behind you.

The Beatty house is huge, and so is the dark musty basement. As you blindly stumble forward, you hope you can find a way out.

THE END

from page 109

You call Tiny, who was just about to leave his house to come watch the race. He agrees to come meet you.

Even though you have enlisted the aid of your big friend, you realize that you are going to have your hands full. You know from the scene in the warehouse that there are many men involved in the plot to steal the head.

But you do have some important knowledge. You know the men plan to hide the head in a backpack as they join the end of the marathon race. Then they will enter the fake ambulance and attempt to make their escape.

You and Tiny decide to stay close to the ambulance. At the moment Mr. Imir and the other runner approach the ambulance, you and Tiny will have a choice. If there are police nearby, you will ask them for help. But most of the police, you notice, are not near the medical tent. They are positioned near the finish line, to help control the huge crowd waiting there for the lead runners to arrive.

When the two runners in combat uniforms approach the ambulance, you and Tiny are on your own. No police officers are nearby. Now you really have to be careful. The other men you saw in the warehouse are in on the plot. Surely some of them will be near the first-aid tent.

As the runners approach the ambulance, you and Tiny go into action. Unfortunately, you are outnumbered. At least ten men surround you and knock you both out.

Later, from your cots in the medical tent, you and Tiny explain to Lieutenant Duffy how you tried to catch the criminals on your own. By now the race is over, the men are gone, and so is the head of Ha-tep.

The lieutenant just shakes his head.

You won't have an easy time, either, explaining to your news editor why you didn't get your story on the marathon.

THE END

from page 99

Covering the upcoming marathon has inspired you more than you realize. Without a moment's hesitation, you jump off the stoop and dash away, feeling as if you could win any race in the world.

As soon as you get to the end of the block, you turn around to make sure that Mr. Imir or one of his henchmen isn't following you.

The coast is clear. But what do you do now?

You've had enough excitement for one day, you decide. It's time you began concentrating on covering the marathon race for the school paper. For your investigation, this is . . .

THE END

from page 109

You call Lieutenant Duffy and tell him your theory, including how Mr. Imir and his men will use the false ambulance for their escape. He believes your story, for your evidence is solid.

Lieutenant Duffy alerts his officers, both in uniform and in plain clothes, and tells them to stake out the race course. As the marathon begins, and the runners pound down the opening stretch of the course, the lieutenant and his officers stay in touch with each other by means of walkie-talkies and beeper phones.

Though the lieutenant has a few officers staked out around the fake ambulance, he concentrates most of his force at the museum itself. It would be standard police procedure to stop the crime from being committed and to try to make the arrests at that time.

From a hiding place in the museum gallery, you and the lieutenant watch as the police guard at the Ha-tep case is called away by an alarm in another part of the building. When two men in army fatigues reach into the case, police appear from everywhere. Mr. Imir and his accomplice are arrested, and other police pick up the man who set off the alarm that lured away the guard.

To your surprise, you share the spotlight with the lieutenant at a news conference. "This alert young reporter is the one who prevented the crime," Lieutenant Duffy tells the news reporters. Later in the day you see yourself on television, standing beside the lieutenant. You have solved the marathon-race mystery.

THE END

from page 109

Taking action alone, you edge your way to the fake ambulance and await the attempted escape. When the two runners in combat uniforms finally arrive, you know you've got them. There are no police officers in sight, so you must go it alone.

"Halt!" you say with authority. "I know what you've got there, so give it up."

"Outta the way," Milo says as he pushes you aside.

Then, before you can shout for help, you're out like a light.

As far as you know, you were hit by *ten* heads of Ha-tep, all at the same time.

Afterwards, you try to explain all this to the lieutenant.

As you watch the unhappy look on the lieutenant's face, you realize that this has not been one of your most successful cases.

THE END

from page 103

When the meeting breaks up, you cautiously follow Mr. Imir out of the Dixie Warehouse. In the back of the building, alongside heaps of rusty metal and broken glass, is a shiny new sports car. Imir walks up to it and sits on the hood. He takes out what appears to be a map. A map of the marathon racecourse? He studies it carefully, making little notations on it as he goes.

When he is finished reading, he folds the paper and places it back in his jacket pocket, laughing heartily to himself. Getting off the hood, Mr. Imir unlocks the door to the sports car, gets in, and starts the motor. He's going to drive away! With your bicycle back at the museum, you'll never be able to follow him. Dead end.

All you can do now is hurry to Smith's Garage.

Turn to page 106.

from page 47

You decide that confronting the uncle and telling him everything you know is the best approach. When you arrive at Peter's apartment, you immediately sit down with the uncle and begin speaking directly and urgently.

The uncle listens to you without comment. You do your best to convince him that he needs help. Finally, he shakes his head.

"I will not call the police. I'm afraid for Peter."

"Then can I help you? How many times have you talked to the kidnappers?" you ask.

"Twice."

"And have they put Peter on the phone?"

"Yes. Both times," says the uncle.

"What did he say?" you ask.

"For me to get the money."

"But they dropped him off on the street before. I was there," you say.

"He did keep saying not to be *alarmed.* That was one word he used over and over again. He said they let him go before only so that he could withdraw from the race. They said if he didn't return to them they would not only kill him when they found him again, but me as well."

Well, that explains why they let Peter go for a while, and why he returned to them. But what about "alarmed"? Why did Peter keep using that word?

You've got it! Peter's not only a marathon runner, he's also the curator of the museum. They want information about the alarms in the museum! The race must just be a cover for a very different kind of crime.

"Anything else? Can you remember anything else about the phone calls? A clue of any sort?" you ask.

"There was one thing," says the uncle. "A noise. Both times Peter was on the phone, I could hear a noise. Like a train."

"Like a train?" you ask. "Do you think it *was* a train?"

"I think it could have been. Yes."

"Do you remember the exact times of day that Peter called? That would be very helpful."

The uncle explains. The kidnappers had called twice. The first time was to tell him that they had Peter, and that if he notified the police, Peter would be killed. They told the uncle to get small bills together, one hundred thousand dollars worth, and to await instructions. Then they put Peter on the phone. Peter pleaded with his uncle to do as the kidnappers wished. It was then that the uncle had heard the sound of a train.

The second call came after the uncle returned from the bank. The uncle told the kidnappers he had the money. Again, they put Peter on the phone, and again the uncle heard the noise of what sounded like a train.

Peter's uncle estimates the time of the train noises at 10:10 A.M. and 2:45 P.M.

Now you have an important clue, or pair of clues: the sound of a train at two different times. But if you are going to do something, you must do it quickly. The second time they called, the kidnappers said they would call again at 5:00 P.M., to tell the uncle when and where to leave the money. So you don't have a minute to lose.

A plan forms in your mind: You could go with Peter's uncle. After he drops off the money, you might be able to follow the kidnappers, and they would lead you to Peter. The uncle has made you promise that you will not call the police. So the question is, should you act alone or should you get your friend Tiny to help you?

If you think you should try to track down Peter alone, turn to page 63.

If you want to get Tiny to help, turn to page 58.